WE DIDN'T MEAN TO GO TO SEA
Stage 4

John, Susan, Titty, and Roger are very happy when their new friend Jim Brading invites them to go sailing on his yacht, the *Goblin*. They all love ships and the sea. Mother is a little worried about the plan, but Jim and the four children promise to stay on the river and not to sail out into the open sea.

But Jim forgets to buy petrol for the ship's engine. He leaves the children on the *Goblin*, safely anchored in the harbour, while he goes ashore to buy some. He'll only be ten minutes. But he doesn't come back. The fog comes down and the tide rises, pulling the anchor off the bottom. Now the *Goblin* is drifting – drifting out of the harbour. Night is falling and with it comes a wind – a wild wind and a stormy sea . . .

It is impossible to turn back, and dangerous to go on.

Arthur Ransome was born in 1884 in Leeds and died in 1967. He was a journalist and writer, and travelled widely in Russia, China and Egypt. His most famous books are the *Swallows and Amazons* series, including *We Didn't Mean to Go to Sea*. Before writing this story, he made the journey himself, sailing his own boat across the North Sea to Holland and back.

OXFORD BOOKWORMS
Series Editor: Jennif

D1513740

OXFORD BOOKWORMS

For a full list of titles in all the Oxford Bookworms series,
please refer to the *Oxford English* catalogue.

～ Green Series ～

Adaptations of classic and modern stories for younger readers.
Titles available include:

Stage 2 (700 headwords)
*Robinson Crusoe *Daniel Defoe*
*Alice's Adventures in Wonderland *Lewis Carroll*
Huckleberry Finn *Mark Twain*
*Anne of Green Gables *L. M. Montgomery*
A Stranger at Green Knowe *Lucy M. Boston*
Too Old to Rock and Roll *Jan Mark* (short stories)

Stage 3 (1000 headwords)
*The Prisoner of Zenda *Anthony Hope*
*The Secret Garden *Frances Hodgson Burnett*
The Railway Children *Edith Nesbit*
On the Edge *Gillian Cross*
'Who, Sir? Me, Sir?' *K.M. Peyton*

Stage 4 (1400 headwords)
*Treasure Island *Robert Louis Stevenson*
*Gulliver's Travels *Jonathan Swift*
A Tale of Two Cities *Charles Dickens*
The Silver Sword *Ian Serraillier*
The Eagle of the Ninth *Rosemary Sutcliff*
We Didn't Mean to go to Sea *Arthur Ransome*

～ Black Series ～

Younger readers might also like to try some of the original stories
from the main Bookworms list. Suggested titles:

Stage 1 (400 headwords)
*The Elephant Man *Tim Vicary*
Under the Moon *Rowena Akinyemi*
*The Phantom of the Opera *Jennifer Bassett*

Stage 2 (700 headwords)
*Voodoo Island *Michael Duckworth*
Ear-rings from Frankfurt *Reg Wright*
*Dead Man's Island *John Escott*

Stage 3 (1000 headwords)
*Skyjack! *Tim Vicary*
The Star Zoo *Harry Gilbert*
Chemical Secret *Tim Vicary*

*Cassettes available for these titles.

We Didn't Mean to Go to Sea

Arthur Ransome

retold by
Ralph Mowat

Illustrated by
Henry Brighouse

OXFORD UNIVERSITY PRESS
1995

Oxford University Press,
Walton Street, Oxford OX2 6DP

Oxford New York
Athens Auckland Bangkok Bombay
Calcutta Cape Town Dar es Salaam Delhi
Florence Hong Kong Istanbul Karachi
Kuala Lumpur Madras Madrid Melbourne
Mexico City Nairobi Paris Singapore
Taipei Tokyo Toronto
and associated companies in
Berlin Ibadan

OXFORD and OXFORD ENGLISH
are trade marks of Oxford University Press

ISBN 0 19 422735 9

First published 1995

Original edition © Arthur Ransome 1937
First published by Jonathan Cape 1937
This simplified edition © Oxford University Press 1995

Typeset by Wyvern Typesetting Ltd, Bristol
Printed in England by Clays Ltd, St Ives plc

1
On the river

John rowed the small boat slowly across the river. Susan and Titty sat together in the stern and Roger, the youngest, was in the bows. Everything on the river was new to them. They had arrived at Pin Mill yesterday and all morning they had watched the boats on the river. Now, at last, they had an old rowing boat and were on the water among the other boats on the wide river.

'It's almost like being at sea,' said Titty.

'I wish we were,' said Roger.

The tide was going out and John had to row a little harder.

'Be careful,' said Susan. 'Don't hit that black buoy. It's

'Don't hit that black buoy,' said Susan.

MAST→

THE GOBLIN

MAINSAIL

STAYSAIL

DECK CABIN COCKPIT TILLER

BOWS STERN

got the name of a boat written on it.'

'*Goblin*,' said Roger. 'Funny name for a boat.'

'There's a boat coming up the river now,' said John.

A little white yacht with red sails was coming in towards the crowd of boats around them. A young man was busy at the mast. They saw the tall red mainsail come down and fall on top of the cabin.

'There's no one at the tiller,' said John.

'The boat's coming straight for us. He's all alone. This must be his buoy,' cried Titty.

'Look out, John!' cried Susan. 'We'll be right in his way.'

John rowed away from the black buoy in the water and they watched as the little yacht came towards them. Slowly and more slowly it moved against the falling tide. Suddenly the young man ran forward and reached down to catch the top of the buoy. But just at that moment the yacht stopped, and immediately the tide began to carry the little boat down the river, away from the buoy.

The young man looked around. 'Hi! You!' he shouted. 'Can you fix a rope to that buoy?'

'Aye, aye, Sir!' shouted John, and a moment later the rope flew through the air. John caught it and gave the end to Roger. 'Pass the rope through the eye on top, Roger.'

'Aye, aye, Sir,' said Roger, and in a moment the rope was tied safely to the buoy. The young man immediately began to pull the rope very hard and the *Goblin* stopped moving down river with the tide. Very soon she was safely moored to the buoy.

'That was very good work. Thank you very much,' said the young man. 'I'm glad you know how to tie a rope.'

'Father taught us,' said John. 'He's in the Navy.'

'Lucky for me,' said the captain of the *Goblin*. 'You saved me from getting into real trouble just then.' He began to put away all the sails and ropes, and to make everything tidy.

'Would you like me to help you put everything away?'

said John, hoping very much that the young man would invite him on board.

'Yes, please,' said the young man. 'You can all come. There's plenty of work for everybody.' And in a moment all four children were in the cockpit of the *Goblin*.

'I say, just look inside,' said Titty.

They looked down into the cabin of the little ship, with beds on each side of a small table.

'I've just got to wash the cups and plates,' said the young captain, 'and then I'll go and have breakfast.'

'BREAKFAST!' Susan, Titty and Roger all said together. 'But it's nearly seven o'clock in the evening. Haven't you eaten anything all day?'

'Not much. Only some soup and a sandwich since I left Dover at two o'clock yesterday afternoon.'

'Have you been sailing alone all night?' said Roger.

'Yes, that's right,' said the young man. 'Look, what are your names? Mine's Jim Brading.'

'Walker,' said John. 'This is Susan, and this is Titty. I'm John . . .'

'And I'm Roger. I say, does your engine really work?'

'It works very well,' said Jim Brading, 'but I never use it if I can use sails.'

'Oh,' said Roger, who was very interested in engines.

By now they were all in the cabin, helping Jim Brading to wash and put away the plates.

'We only arrived here yesterday,' said John. 'To meet Daddy at Harwich. He's coming home from China and

4

he's going to work near here, at Shotley.'

'Mother and Bridget, our little sister, are here, too,' added Susan. 'We're staying with Miss Powell at Alma Cottage.'

'Do you live in the *Goblin* all the time?' asked Titty.

'Wish I did, but I've just finished school. I'm going to Oxford University in another month. I'll live in the *Goblin* till then. My uncle's coming on Monday and we're going to sail to Scotland.'

'We've sailed in an open boat,' said John. 'But we've never had one that we could sleep in.'

'Like to spend a night in the *Goblin*?' said Jim.

'Oh yes!' said everyone at once.

'We'd love to, if only we could,' said Susan.

At that moment they heard voices outside.

'They'll be on this yacht here, Ma'am. There's their rowing boat tied up behind.' It was Frank, the boatman.

'Oh!' said Susan. 'Mother's had to come and look for us.' They all climbed out of the cabin into the cockpit of the *Goblin*.

Mrs Walker spoke to Jim Brading. 'I hope my children haven't given you any trouble.'

'They've helped me a lot,' said Jim, 'and I've been very glad to have them.'

'His name's Jim Brading,' said Roger, 'and he's sailed by himself from Dover, since yesterday.'

'He hasn't even had *breakfast* yet,' said Titty.

Mother looked at Jim. She knew very well what her

children wanted. 'Our supper is waiting for us,' she said, smiling. 'If Jim would like to come, you'd better bring him with you.'

'Do come,' said Susan. 'We'd all like you to.'

'Thank you,' said Jim. 'That's very good of you.'

Mrs Walker went on first to tell Miss Powell that they had a visitor.

'Well, Jim,' said Miss Powell when they arrived. 'You need a bit of sleep by the look of you.'

'I didn't have any sleep last night,' said Jim. 'How are you, Miss Powell?'

'Do you know him?' asked Titty, surprised.

Miss Powell laughed. 'Know Jim Brading? I should think I do. I've known him since he was a child.'

'Sh! Don't wake him!'

Mother came into a room that was strangely silent. Susan was standing by her chair, holding a finger to her lips. And Jim Brading was fast asleep. He had sat down and his head had dropped lower and lower until it was resting on the table.

'He's tired out,' whispered Susan.

John watched. So that was how you felt after sailing all night, alone, in a ship of your own. How soon would he have a ship himself?

Miss Powell laughed quietly when she came in.

'He'll be all right when he's had a bit of food.'

Jim Brading was fast asleep.

Suddenly Jim Brading moved and nearly knocked over a glass. He lifted his head and stared about him.

'Oh, I say . . . I'm terribly sorry . . . I didn't mean to . . . How long have I been asleep?'

'It's all right,' said Mother. 'I know just how you feel. You'll feel better when you've had some soup.'

And really, it was a very nice thing to happen. You can't

7

think of someone as a stranger when you've seen him asleep on your dinner table. Jim Brading had become one of the family. While they were eating, they asked him lots of questions, but not another word was said about them spending a night in the *Goblin*. They were beginning to think he had forgotten, and then, suddenly, the offer was made again, and Mother was there to hear it.

'What are you going to do until your uncle comes?'

'Wait around for him,' said Jim. 'But look, I meant what I said earlier. Why don't you come with me for a few days? I can find room for you . . .'

'Sleeping on a ship,' said Titty. 'Oh, Mother . . .'

'They'd love it, of course,' said Mother, 'but I can't let them go just now. Their father's on his way home and we've come to meet him at Harwich. I can't meet him and tell him that most of his family's gone off to sea.'

'I wouldn't take them to sea,' said Jim. 'Just on the rivers and Harwich harbour. There's plenty to see.'

'I say, Mother, couldn't we?' said John.

'Just for a few days,' said Titty.

'If you say when you want them back,' said Jim, 'I'll promise to get them back to Pin Mill in plenty of time.'

'I'm not sure, so I'm going to think about it,' said Mother. 'And Mr Brading must think about it, too. He may wake up in the morning and not like the idea.'

'Oh, Mother!' said Susan, who had not said a word till then.

'No, Susan,' said Mother firmly. 'Mr Brading's tired and

he should be in bed asleep now. And so should Bridget. We'll talk about it again in the morning.'

The next morning the children saw that Mother's bedroom door was open, but there was no one inside.

'Mother's gone out,' cried Roger, who was at the window and could see Mother walking back to the house. They ran out to meet her.

'Hallo,' she said. 'I've been asking people about that young man. Everybody seems to think well of him. Frank, the boatman, says he knows everything there is to know about sailing and small boats.'

'You're going to let us go?' said John.

'Perhaps Jim won't want you today, after a night's sleep,' replied Mother, 'but if he does, I suppose . . . But I wonder what your father would say.'

'Daddy'd say "Go . . ."'

'I believe he would,' said Mother.

They looked out at the white *Goblin* on the calm water of the river. There was no sign of life.

'He's still asleep,' said Mother. 'Let's have breakfast.'

Before they finished breakfast, Jim Brading arrived.

'I'm terribly sorry, Mrs Walker, about the way I fell asleep on your table last night.'

'Don't apologize,' said Mother. 'It was a natural thing to do. Come and sit down. Well, now you've seen these animals in the morning light, I'm sure you don't want four of them in your little ship. I've told them you won't, so don't be afraid that they'll be disappointed.'

'How soon can they come aboard?' said Jim.

Five hours later John, Susan and Jim Brading were resting in the cockpit of the *Goblin* after a hard morning's work. Mrs Walker and the others had gone into Ipswich to get food. It had been a busy morning, bringing all the blankets and other things they would need to live and sleep on board the *Goblin*. When everything had been put into the little cabin, there was no room left for people. But Susan found a place for everything, and the next time John and Jim looked, the cabin looked empty, and very tidy.

'You'd better learn the ropes,' said Jim, and he and John spent the next hour putting up the mainsail and bringing it down again. The third time John was able to do it alone. Jim explained the other things that John needed to know about the *Goblin*'s different sails and ropes. There were more ropes than in the little boats that John had sailed before, but after a while he began to understand how everything worked and was able to make himself useful.

When Mother came back from Ipswich with Titty and Roger, they brought a lot of food, and Susan put it all away in the cupboards in the cabin.

'Jim,' said Mother, 'have you got any charts? Show me where you're going to go.'

Jim brought out his chart of Harwich harbour.

'This is where we are now,' he said, putting his finger on the chart. 'That's Pin Mill, and this is the river going up to Ipswich. The other way, the river goes down to meet the River Stour at Shotley. The two rivers together make Harwich harbour, and this buoy, the Beach End buoy, shows where the harbour ends and the sea begins.'

'And you won't go out past that buoy?' said Mother.

'No,' said Jim. 'We shan't go out of the harbour.'

'And you'll come back the day after tomorrow,' said Mother to her children. 'You don't want to miss Daddy.'

'We promise,' they all said.

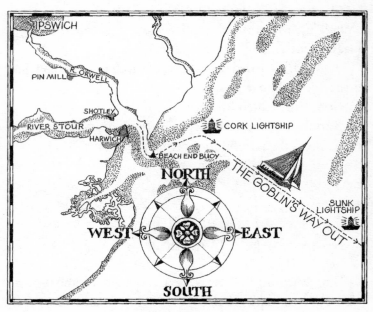

Chart of Harwich harbour

11

'I promise, too,' said Jim. 'I'll make sure they're here at Pin Mill on Friday in time for tea.'

'That's all right,' said Mother. 'Have a good time. And if you stop at Shotley, or anywhere else, try to telephone me at Miss Powell's.'

Mother and Bridget climbed down into the old rowing boat and the *Goblin* got ready to sail. The mainsail was pulled up and began to fill in the wind. John stood ready to untie the rope to the buoy.

'Let go now,' called Jim, and John dropped the *Goblin*'s buoy back into the water.

'All gone, Sir!' shouted John.

'Pull up the staysail,' called Jim. 'Pull on that rope, Susan. That's right. We're sailing.'

The *Goblin* turned round in the water and moved faster as the wind filled her sails.

'Goodbye,' called Mother and Bridget, waving.

'Goodbye,' shouted the crew of the *Goblin* as she sailed away down the river in the warm afternoon sunshine.

2
In harbour

They were off. There were a few busy moments with ropes and sails, but now the *Goblin* was sailing gently down the river and the four children began to talk again.

'Two days ago,' said Titty quietly, 'we were in the train, coming to Pin Mill.'

'I was outside Dover, wishing for wind,' laughed Jim.

'And now we're all here,' said Titty and Susan.

'You steer *Goblin*, John, while I go and tidy up on deck,' said Jim.

'Are you sure I can?' said John, looking worried.

'Of course you can. Just keep her as she's going.'

The tiller was in John's hands. Susan and Titty were watching him. Could he do it? The children were only used to a small sailing boat, and this yacht was much bigger. But it was not nearly as hard as John had thought, and soon he began to feel more confident.

Jim came back into the cockpit, and John moved along so that Jim could sit down and take the tiller.

'No, you carry on,' said Jim. 'You're doing well.'

On they went. Soon the river became wider and they sailed into Harwich harbour.

'Now then,' said Jim. 'Susan, why not give John a rest, and let's see how you can steer.'

Susan sat down beside John and took the tiller. There was only one thought in her mind; she must keep the *Goblin* sailing straight and keep her sails full of wind. But suddenly Roger jumped up on one of the seats in the cockpit, pointing with his finger and shouting.

'Look! Look! It's a black pig, swimming.'

'Where?' shouted Titty.

'There. No, it's gone now. No. Look! There it is!'

13

'It's a porpoise,' said Jim. 'They like swimming around boats.'

Porpoises were too much, even for Susan. She stopped thinking about keeping the *Goblin* sailing straight and looked for the porpoise.

'Look out for your steering,' said John.

'It's a porpoise,' said Jim.

14

'Sorry,' said Susan as she felt the wind pull on the sails. 'All right, John, I won't look again.'

'Where are we going to anchor for the night?' Roger asked.

'I know a good place,' said Jim. 'Off Shotley Pier – we can go ashore and telephone your mother.'

The wind had dropped and the tide was against them as they came to the place where Jim wanted to anchor.

'Only just enough wind,' said Jim. 'I'll go forward and get the anchor ready.'

'Can I come and see how you do it?' asked John.

Susan, Titty and Roger were left alone in the cockpit. Susan was steering and the *Goblin* slowly came closer to the pier. John watched carefully as Jim held the anchor over the bows, ready to drop it into the water.

'Now, bring the sails down,' Jim called to the others, and he let the anchor fall into the water. The *Goblin* stopped.

'We've arrived,' said Titty. 'Let's go ashore.'

'Let's have supper first,' said Susan.

'Tell us about your voyage from Dover,' said John, as they were finishing supper.

'Nothing much to tell,' said Jim, 'except that when you're sailing alone, you can't have any sleep. I had to wait quite a long time outside the entrance to the harbour here. There are a lot of shoals outside; you know, places where the water is very shallow, and it's very easy to run aground.

Jim held the anchor over the bows.

There was a bit of fog, and I didn't want to try to find my way into the harbour until I could see the buoys. I don't like shoals; they're very dangerous.'

'Where are the shoals outside Harwich?' asked John.

'Look at the chart,' replied Jim. There's Harwich, and there's Shotley, where we are now,' and he pointed with his finger. 'And all the shoals are just outside. The big ships like to come in like this,' and his finger followed a safe line between the shoals. 'They go towards the *Cork* lightship. It's the only safe way to go. And when it's dark, or foggy, the only safe thing to do is to get out to sea and stay there.'

John listened, telling himself he would remember that, when one day he had a boat of his own.

'What did you do?' asked Roger.

'Just sailed about, outside all of the shoals. Then, in the morning I came to the *Sunk* lightship, then the *Cork*, and then to the Beach End buoy – you'll see that tomorrow –

16

and into the harbour and up to Pin Mill. And when I got there, some very good young sailors helped me to tie up to my buoy. Now, it's nearly nine o'clock, and time to go and tell your mother you haven't drowned.'

When they came back to the *Goblin*, it was nearly dark, and it was time for Susan, Titty and Roger to go to bed. They looked at all the other boats with their lights shining softly across the calm waters of the harbour. A few minutes later John and Jim went to bed, too.

They slept. The night was so calm that it was hard to believe that they were sleeping on a boat. But when they had been asleep for about an hour, they were reminded that they were very near the open sea. A small noise got louder and louder, and soon the *Goblin* was rolling violently from side to side. Everybody woke up suddenly.

'What's happened?' called Roger.

'It's all right,' said Jim. 'It's a big ship going out to sea. There's one that goes across to Holland every night. I forgot to tell you about it.'

'One day soon it'll bring Daddy back from Holland,' said Titty, as the *Goblin* stopped rolling about. A few minutes later all was quiet again. The crew of the *Goblin* were asleep.

At seven o'clock the next morning the sleepy crew were woken by a loud shout into the cabin.

'Come on, then. Anybody want a swim before breakfast?

We've got no time to lose before the tide turns.' Jim was already in the cockpit, ready for a swim. The others hurried to join him.

Later on, after the swim, Susan found that Jim was in a hurry to set sail and they had no time for breakfast. They were off, sailing down with the tide towards the entrance to the harbour, and the crew ate some of their breakfast while the *Goblin* sailed slowly past the town of Harwich. There was very little wind and the sails moved lazily from one side to the other.

'Later on,' said Jim, 'there'll be wind. Or fog. Or both. You never know with a day that starts like this.'

As he spoke, they heard the long, loud sound of the *Cork* lightship outside the harbour entrance, which meant that there was fog out at sea. The tide was going out fast and it carried the *Goblin* towards the place where the harbour ends and the sea begins.

'Are we going right down to the last buoy?' asked Roger.

'I promised your mother that we wouldn't go further,' said Jim.

The Goblin *sailed slowly past the town of Harwich.*

Then they heard another sound, like a deep bell.

'That's the Beach End buoy,' said Jim. 'Time to turn back.'

But there was no wind at all to bring them back, and the tide continued to carry the *Goblin* towards the Beach End buoy and the open sea.

'All right,' said Jim, 'we've got to use the engine.'

'Can I be engineer?' asked Roger.

'All right, Roger. Start the engine.'

Nearer and nearer came the sound of the Beach End buoy, but soon they heard the sound of the engine. Quickly the *Goblin* turned and began to move slowly against the tide.

'What happens if the engine doesn't start?' asked Titty.

'Without the engine, we would just go on out to sea,' said Jim. 'Not far, because the tide'll turn soon and bring us back. But I promised your mother we wouldn't go outside the harbour.'

'We all promised,' said Susan, looking back over the stern of the boat to where the Beach End buoy was now lost in the fog. From further out at sea came the long, low sound, 'Beu . . . eueueueueu . . .' of the foghorn on the *Cork* lightship.

'I'm very glad the engine started,' she went on. 'And now I'm going to cook the rest of breakfast.'

Already the *Goblin* was moving away from the mouth of the harbour. Roger looked down into the cabin where Susan was cooking eggs. Suddenly they looked at each other. The noise of the engine was changing, becoming slower, and then it stopped completely. For a moment there was silence.

Jim jumped into the cockpit and looked into the engine.

'No petrol,' he said. 'What a stupid thing to do! I forgot to fill up before we started. Keep going straight ahead, John. We'll anchor over there; it's quite shallow near that buoy.' The *Goblin* was still going forward, but already more slowly. Jim ran forward and they heard the noise of the anchor chain as he got it ready and dropped the anchor into the water.

'What are we going to do?' asked Roger.

'Wait for wind,' said John.

'Get some petrol,' said Jim. 'I'll row ashore and, if I can catch that bus over there, I'll be back in ten minutes. You're in charge, John. Don't let anybody fall overboard. It's low water now, the tide's just turning. You'll be all right here. Nothing can possibly happen.'

The four Walker children watched Jim row the *Goblin*'s little black boat towards the shore. Susan suddenly remembered the eggs and called the others down to breakfast. It was ten past eight.

'I'll keep Jim's eggs warm,' said Susan.

Two hours passed, and Jim's breakfast still waited for him in the cabin. The crew were all on deck.

'What's happened to him?' said Susan. 'It's getting quite foggy now, even in the harbour.'

There was no doubt about it. Fog was coming in from

Jim's breakfast still waited for him in the cabin.

the sea with the tide, and it was already difficult to see where the land ended and the sea began at the mouth of the harbour. Four times every minute the foghorn from the *Cork* lightship sounded out at sea. And then, suddenly, the fog was all around them.

'I can't see the land,' said Roger.

'Oh, John, what are we going to do?' said Susan in a worried voice. 'It's half past eleven. Jim will never find the *Goblin* in this fog.'

'He'll wait,' said John, 'until the fog clears.'

Hours went by, and the fog was just as thick. The children got themselves a meal, and tried not to worry. They heard ships' bells banging in the harbour, and the

21

horns of ships going up the river, but whichever way they looked, they could see nothing except grey fog.

'I can't stop thinking that something terrible's happened to Jim,' said Susan. 'It's two o'clock – six hours since he went.'

'High tide,' said John. 'The fog will probably go out when the tide turns. We're all right here, anchored in a safe place. And Jim knows that. Nothing can possibly go wrong. He said so himself.'

And then Susan saw John's eyes suddenly open very wide. They had both heard the noise of the anchor chain.

'Oh, it's all right,' said John. 'The tide is beginning to turn and go out now, and the *Goblin* is just moving around with the tide.'

But a few moments later the noise came again, with a sudden movement of the whole ship. Then there was another sharp movement, and John jumped up to run to the bows.

'She's pulling her anchor off the bottom,' he cried.

3

Drifting out to sea

As John ran to the *Goblin*'s bows, he looked around in the fog. He could see nothing; he could not even be sure that the *Goblin* was still in the same place. What had happened? How could the *Goblin* pull the anchor from the bottom of the harbour?

And then he remembered. When Jim had gone for petrol, the tide was out; the water was shallow. Now, six hours later, it was high tide again, and the water under the *Goblin* was much deeper. The anchor chain was now far too short to reach the bottom.

John felt terribly ashamed. Why hadn't he thought of that? Why hadn't he let out more chain a long time ago? He looked at the chain. It was kept in a box under the deck. It came out through a hole in the deck and went down into the water. All he had to do was pull more chain out of the box. He pulled, and nothing happened; he pulled again, and suddenly the chain came quickly, out of the box and over the side, into the water. There was nothing to stop it. John put his foot on the chain, but it was too heavy, and it was going too fast. John fell over, on to his back. Before he could get up again, he saw the end of the chain disappear over the side of the *Goblin* and fall into the water. Then there was silence.

'Beu . . . eueueueu . . .' came the sound of the *Cork* lightship, but on the *Goblin* there was a frightened silence. The crew knew that something terrible had happened. Susan came hurrying along the deck.

'Have you hurt yourself?' she asked.

'It's all gone! It's all gone!' was all that John could say. 'All his chain and anchor – I've lost it all!'

'But are you all right?' said Susan.

23

'Chain and anchor, everything,' said John. 'It's all gone.'

'John,' cried Susan. 'We're adrift!' And then, at the top of her voice she shouted, 'Jim! Help! Help!'

'Shut up!' shouted John angrily. 'He can't hear you! Quick! We've got to get the other anchor into the water.' He looked at the second anchor which lay in two pieces on the deck. 'Get some rope while I get the anchor ready.'

The second anchor, called a 'kedge' anchor, was in two parts which had to be fixed together. John wasn't sure how to do it, and it wasn't easy, but when Susan came back with a long piece of rope, he was ready.

John fixed the rope very, very carefully to the kedge anchor; he didn't want to lose two of Jim's anchors. It was

The 'kedge' anchor was in two parts.

24

heavy, too heavy for John alone. Together he and Susan let it fall slowly into the water. A moment later the *Goblin* seemed to stop moving.

'I don't know how far we've moved,' said John. 'You can't tell in the fog. I don't know where we are now.'

'Oh, I wish Jim had never gone ashore,' said Susan. 'He would know what to do.'

'We can't do anything about that,' replied John. 'We've just got to take care of the *Goblin* and make sure nothing else goes wrong.'

'Bang! . . . Bang!' The noise of a bell surprised them. It seemed quite near, but they couldn't see anything in the fog.

'What's that?' called Roger.

'Another boat, probably,' said Susan.

'Bang! . . . Bang!'

'It's like the bell we heard this morning,' said John. 'You know, on that buoy we passed in the harbour.'

'It's nearer than it was,' said Titty.

'Bang! . . . Bang!'

'It must be a boat,' said Roger.

John didn't really hear them. The *Goblin* was moving again with the water. What had gone wrong with the anchor? He hurried back to the bows and saw that the rope was hanging straight down into the water. Desperately he began to pull it in.

'What's happened?' asked Susan, coming up behind him.

'The anchor isn't holding on the bottom of the sea. Something's wrong with it. Look, here it comes.'

Together they pulled the kedge anchor on to the deck.

'Oh, look. The two pieces aren't fixed together. That's why the anchor didn't hold.'

'John! John! It's here . . .' came a shout from the cockpit.

Suddenly, out of the fog came a large, round buoy. Inside it was the bell – big and black.

'Bang! . . . Bang!'

As the tide pulled them past it, they read the big white letters on the side of the buoy . . . 'BEACH END'. A moment later the buoy was behind them, and the next 'Bang!' was not so loud.

'Oh, John!' cried Susan. 'That was the Beach End buoy. We're out at sea!'

'The Beach End buoy . . . Out at sea . . .'

Titty and Roger stared at each other in the cockpit. They had heard Susan say it. They had seen the big buoy and its bell. And now it was behind them. They weren't safely anchored in Harwich harbour. They were out at sea.

'What's John doing?' said Roger.

'I think they're putting the anchor down again,' said Titty. She could see John, on his knees, in the bows.

'It's no good,' they heard Susan say.

'The water's too deep,' said John. 'We can't stop her.' Hurriedly they began to pull the rope up again.

'That was the Beach End buoy. We're out at sea!'

'They seem awfully worried,' said Titty, watching from the cockpit. 'Which way is the land?'

'Over there . . .' said Roger.

'No, it can't be. It was on the other side a moment ago. I could hear the noise of a train.'

'John,' called Roger. 'Why are all the noises moving round?'

'The *Goblin*'s turning round and round in the tide,' came the answer. 'Because we're drifting.'

'She going up and down quite a lot,' said Roger.

'Yes,' replied Titty. She had noticed that, too. She also knew that she felt different. The bigger waves of the sea made the *Goblin* move much more than in the calm water in the harbour. She couldn't see so well, and her head felt rather strange.

Susan came back to the cockpit, holding on carefully to the wood on top of the cabin. She, too, had noticed how the movement had changed. John had gone into the cabin to look at the chart. He put it on the table.

'That's where we were anchored,' he said, pointing with a finger. 'And there's the Beach End buoy. We must be drifting towards the lightship.' He remembered what Jim had said about shoals. 'Get out to sea and stay there.' That was what Jim had said. He wished desperately that Jim was aboard. Where was the safe way through the shoals? What had Jim said? Was it by the *Cork* lightship? It must be here, and John put his finger on what looked like a wide, clear road leading out, between the shoals, to deep water.

Just at that moment a lot of noises came together. There was the 'Beu . . . eueueu' of the lightship, a sudden loud noise from the *Goblin*'s own foghorn that Roger had found in the cockpit, and then a shout from Titty.

'There's another buoy!'

'Where? Where?' shouted Susan.

John jumped up the steps out of the cabin.

'It's gone. It was over there,' said Titty.

John looked at the chart again. Buoys meant shoals. And there seemed to be shoals everywhere. What was the right thing to do? What would Jim do?

'There's another buoy! It's going to hit us!' shouted Susan.

John moved the tiller left and right; nothing happened. The *Goblin* was drifting with the tide and he could not steer her.

'Push it away!' he shouted, but it was too late, and they all waited for the crash that might sink the small, helpless yacht.

The crash never came. The *Goblin* turned slowly in the tide, missed the heavy metal buoy by half a metre, and moved past it into the fog.

'Oh John,' cried Susan. 'What can we do?'

John knew he had to decide quickly. 'We can't go on like this. We might hit the next buoy. We've got to put up the sails. Then we can steer.'

'But would Jim want you to do that?'

'It's the only thing to do. We're helpless, drifting like this. We've got to put up the sails.'

From the cockpit they watched John climb carefully along the deck and put up the sails. It wasn't easy. John had done it only once before, with Jim Brading, but the others helped with the ropes and in the end the sails went up quite smoothly. Soon the *Goblin* was sailing and John hurried back to take the tiller.

'Now, we've got to miss the shoals,' he said.

The *Goblin* sailed on into the fog, but Susan was very unhappy. She was thinking of Jim Brading rowing around in the harbour, looking for his yacht. What would he do when he found that the *Goblin* had gone? Telephone to Mother at Pin Mill? Jim Brading would have to tell Mother that he didn't know where they were, and that thought really frightened Susan. They had all promised they wouldn't go out of the harbour. And here they were, in someone else's yacht, sailing in a thick fog, faster and faster away from the land. Their promises had been broken. What was better? To break a promise? Or to put their lives, and the *Goblin*, in danger on the rocks and shoals?

The *Goblin* was going up and down, up and down, much more now they were out at sea. Titty's head was aching, and she was afraid she was going to be sick, but she didn't want anyone else to know. The wind was much stronger than before.

'Look, Susan,' said John. 'We can't go on sailing without knowing where we're going. I've got to look at the chart. You take the tiller while I go down into the cabin.'

But Susan didn't want that.

'You keep the tiller,' she said. 'I'll go down and get the chart.' She climbed down the steps into the cabin, and

The Goblin *was going up and down, up and down.*

almost at once she began to feel worse. There seemed to be no air . . . none at all. 'I'm not going to be seasick!' she said to herself. But she found her mouth open . . . Air . . . That was what she wanted. Quickly she picked up the chart and climbed the steps out of the cabin.

'You haven't hurt yourself, have you?' said Titty.

'I'm all right,' said Susan, taking deep breaths of fresh air. Already she felt better. She heard John talking. What was he saying? No . . . No . . . No . . . He couldn't mean it . . .

'There are shoals all around the lightship. But there's a clear way out to sea. We'll be safe there.'

31

'But we can't . . . We can't.' Susan was close to tears. The loud sound of Roger's foghorn made her put her hands over her ears. But she tried to listen to John.

'We can't stop. Remember what Jim said – "Keep away from shoals. Get out to sea and stay there." That's what he'd do now. And wait until he could see clearly before trying to come back.'

'But we promised not to go out to sea at all,' said Susan unhappily. She could see Titty and Roger looking at her and she turned her head away.

'We didn't want to do it,' said John. 'But we're at sea now, and we can't get back in the fog. We've got to go on.'

'Beu . . . eueueueu . . .' came the sound of the *Cork* lightship.

'It's very near,' said Titty. 'We can't keep a promise that's already broken. Let's do what John says. Daddy would say the same.'

'But how shall we ever get back?' said Susan.

'When the fog clears, we'll be able to turn round, we'll be able to see things, and come back.'

'Beu . . . eueueu . . . eueu . . .'

The *Cork* lightship was now very near indeed, and John knew that there was no time to waste.

'I'm going to take her right out. Come on, Susan. You've got to take the tiller while I make sure we're going the right way.'

For a few minutes Susan held on to the tiller and tried to keep the *Goblin* sailing straight. John looked at the chart

32

and watched the compass carefully. They had to go south-east to keep away from the shoals. Yes, that was it. They had to get past the *Sunk* lightship – outside all the shoals – and then they would be safe. That was where Jim had waited on his way from Dover. He looked at Susan and Titty. Titty's face was green and there were tears running down Susan's face.

'It's all wrong!' she cried. 'We've got to go back. We promised!'

'We can't go back. It isn't safe to try,' said John.

'We must!' said Susan. Roger looked at her. This was a Susan he had never seen. And then Titty suddenly bent over the side of the cockpit.

'She's being sick,' said Roger.

'I'm going into the cabin,' said Titty a few minutes later. 'I'll feel better if I lie down.'

John watched the compass carefully.

33

'Come on, then,' said Susan. 'I'll help you get into bed.' But in the cabin it happened, the thing she had been most afraid of: she felt sick. Could she get out in time? 'Oh . . . Oh . . .' she cried as she climbed up the steps into the cockpit, and almost immediately was sick over the side. She was sick again and again. John looked at his sister and felt terribly sorry for her. Should they go back? Could they go back? He looked behind the *Goblin* into the thick, grey fog. No. The only safe way was to go on.

'Beu . . . eueueu . . .' came the sound of the *Cork* light-ship. But it was behind them now. Before them was the grey curtain of fog. And beyond it was the open sea.

4
A stormy night

The *Goblin* sailed on through the fog. They left the sound of the *Cork* lightship behind them and for a while heard only the wind and the sea. Then a new noise came out of the fog – a long sound, then a pause, then the long sound again, and then silence for a whole minute.

'What is it?' asked Susan.

'It's the next lightship,' said John. 'It must be the *Sunk*, where Jim waited when he was coming from Dover. We've done it, Susan! We're safe outside all the shoals, and we haven't hit anything.'

'But we shouldn't be here at all,' cried Susan. She held her head in her hands and tried not to think about being sick.

The wind was stronger now and the *Goblin* was sailing faster through the fog. Roger sounded the foghorn again, but not as often as before. He wasn't so frightened now. Although Susan and Titty were sick, he and John were all right.

They never saw the *Sunk* lightship. Two hours later the fog began to disappear, but then the rain began. At first it was not too heavy, but very quickly the wind became more violent, and out of the west behind them came a white wall of rain, beating down into the sea. In seconds the red mainsail was black with water, and rivers of rain ran off the cabin roof into the cockpit. It was still too dangerous to think of turning back because they could see nothing through the rain. So they went on, and the wind blew them further and further away from the land.

By the time it stopped raining, the sky in front of them was already growing dark, and the *Goblin* was sailing faster than ever through the white-topped waves.

'Let's turn back now,' said Susan.

John took a deep breath. He wasn't sure that he could find his way back, but he kept his doubts to himself.

'All right,' he said. 'I'll bring the *Goblin* round now. We'll have to pull in the mainsail, so get ready.'

The next moment terrible things began to happen. When you are sailing with the wind, you never really know how hard the wind is blowing. It's very different when you turn against it. As the *Goblin* turned into the wind, the waves threw the little ship on to her side. Susan lost the rope for the mainsail but John managed to catch it and fix the sail. He pulled the tiller round and the *Goblin* turned straight into the wind and the waves.

Crash! A wave broke over the bows, and water flew over the cabin roof and onto the children in the cockpit. Roger was thrown into the bottom of the cockpit and did not even try to get up. Up the *Goblin* came, her bows pointing to the sky, then down again, and another wave thundered over the ship. In the cockpit they were knee-deep in water. John, white-faced and desperate, fought with the tiller and tried to steer against a sea and a wind that were too strong for him.

'Stop it, John! Stop it! We'll have to turn round again! I can't . . . I can't . . . Oh! . . . Oh! . . .' And Susan, shaken almost to pieces by the ship's new violent movement, lay across the side of the cockpit and was terribly sick again.

John tried to find the rope of the mainsail under the water in the cockpit. He found it, lost it, found it again, and then pushed with his whole body against the tiller. Slowly, very slowly, the brave little *Goblin* turned away from the wind and back on her old course. It seemed like a return to peace after a terrible battle.

From the cabin they heard Titty's frightened voice. There was water down there as well as in the cockpit. Roger went down to help her, and Susan looked for the

Another wave thundered over the ship,
and in the cockpit they were knee-deep in water.

pump, found it, and began pumping hard to get the water out of the boat.

But the wind was still very strong, and the *Goblin* was

sailing very fast, too fast. Night was coming, and the wind might get stronger. John was finding it harder and harder to hold the tiller straight, and he knew that he could not go on like this much longer.

'I've got to make the sail smaller,' he shouted to Susan, 'so that we go more slowly. You take the tiller while I go to the mast.'

'You can't go!' cried Susan.

'I've got to,' said John, and tied a rope around his waist. 'That'll keep me safe. If I fall overboard, I can climb back . . . It'll be all right.'

'No! John! No!' shouted Susan, but it was too late. He had already climbed out of the cockpit and was going carefully, very carefully, along the roof of the cabin to the bottom of the mast.

John had never felt so lonely in all his life. The *Goblin* seemed to want to throw him into the sea but he managed to reach the foot of the mast. Then he had to stand up. 'One hand for yourself and one for the ship,' his father had told him years ago. He held on to the mast with one hand and started to roll the sail down. As the sail became smaller, the *Goblin* began to go more slowly. John suddenly felt more confident. He began to turn to go back, and then his foot caught on a rope.

As he fell, he heard Susan scream.

'John! John!' Where was he? Susan looked at the waves going past the cockpit and saw nothing. And then, when she thought he had gone for ever, she saw his hand over the top of the cabin. John was still on board the *Goblin* and he was coming back to the cockpit.

'What happened?' called Roger from the cabin.

'Nothing happened,' said John, climbing down into the cockpit. 'I fell down, that's all. I'm all right now.' But Susan could see that his hands were shaking as he took off the rope that he had tied around his waist.

It began to grow dark and the little world of the *Goblin* seemed even smaller than in the fog. The wind was still blowing hard but the *Goblin* sailed on smoothly. Even Susan began to feel better. Nobody had fallen overboard, and sooner or later the night would end. The sun would rise, the wind would drop, and they would sail back to Harwich. Susan and Titty didn't feel seasick any more. John's arms ached with steering, but he felt much happier. Roger was hungry and wondered if everyone had forgotten about supper.

'Susan,' he said. 'It's ten o'clock. What about some chocolate or something?'

'Ten o'clock,' said Susan in surprise. 'It's time you all had something to eat.' And a few minutes later they were all eating very large pieces of fruit cake.

Suddenly Susan, then Roger, saw lights ahead. 'There's a green light, and a red light on the other side.'

'It must be a big ferry, on its way from Holland to Harwich. It's coming this way,' said John.

'Maybe they could take us back,' said Roger. 'It's getting nearer and nearer. I can see it very clearly.'

'But they can't see us!' shouted John suddenly. 'We've got no lights! And it's coming straight towards us. We've got to get out of the way. We've got to warn them. Roger, sound the foghorn!'

'*The ferry's coming straight towards us!*'

40

Someone on the ferry heard the loud noise of the foghorn, and at the last minute the ferry changed course. The green starboard light of the big ship disappeared and its high black sides went quickly past the *Goblin*. 'Show your lights, you stupid fishermen,' came an angry voice from a loudspeaker above, and then the ferry had passed them and was off on its way to Harwich. The *Goblin*, and everyone in it, was thrown from side to side in the big waves made by the ferry, but they were still in one piece.

Back at Pin Mill Bridget and Mother listened to the wind and the rain during the night.

'I wonder what noises they can hear in the *Goblin*,' said Bridget.

'They're anchored somewhere safe and all asleep,' said Mother. 'And you should be asleep, too.' She tried to keep the worry out of her voice as she listened to the wind and wondered where her children were.

It was a long August night, but in the morning the sun was shining, and when Mother and Bridget came down to breakfast, there was a telegram from Daddy. He had reached Berlin on the train, and would be in England soon.

'Oh dear,' said Mrs Walker. 'If he was in Berlin yesterday, that means he'll probably come across on the ferry to Harwich today. We'll have to go to meet him. But what if the *Goblin* doesn't get back in time?'

41

5
Sinbad and the pilot

Another hour of the night went by and the *Goblin* sailed bravely on through the dark. There had been no more rain, but the wind was still blowing strongly. Susan sent Roger and Titty down to the cabin to sleep and then fell asleep herself in the cockpit, tired out by worry, seasickness, and her terrible fear earlier when John had nearly fallen into the sea.

John held on to the tiller, watched the compass, and tried to stay awake. The movement of the *Goblin* became less violent – the wind was not so strong as before. John began to feel happy. He was alone, in the dark with his ship, sailing across the North Sea. Then he remembered – Mother worrying at Pin Mill, Jim Brading's lost chain and anchor, the journey home again. But then he thought a bit more. The *Goblin* was all right; she hadn't hit any buoys or shoals or ferries. Susan and Titty and Roger were all safe. He had done his best. There was a happy smile on John's face, but nobody to see it. Above him the sky was full of stars, and all around him was the loneliness of the sea.

He was the captain of the *Goblin*; and he would never forget that night.

What was that? Something in the darkness far ahead. John saw a light for a moment, then it was gone, then it came again. It must be a lightship, straight ahead. There would be people there who could help him, who would tell him where he was, who could tell him how to get back to Harwich. He counted the time between the lights as they went off and on . . . off and on.

Suddenly he realized that the sail was making a noise like thunder, and the *Goblin* had turned sideways to the waves and was rolling wildly up and down.

'John! John! What's happened?'

Susan had woken suddenly, and was frightened.

'I fell asleep,' John shouted. 'It'll be all right in a minute.' Slowly he got the *Goblin* back on course and saw the lights of the lightship again.

'You'd better let me steer for a bit,' said Susan. 'You can't go on without sleeping.'

John hesitated. 'See if you can,' he said at last. 'Keep going towards that lightship.'

He sat down in a corner of the cockpit. 'Just for a few minutes,' he said.

His head fell forward, against the cold, wet cabin wall. He let it rest there . . . It wouldn't matter if his eyes closed . . . Just for one minute.

From far, far away John heard someone talking . . . calling his name.

'John! . . . John!' That was Susan's voice. John sat up and stared about him.

'I've been keeping her going south-east,' said Susan, 'but we passed the lightship a long time ago. It's still dark, but

43

there's another light in the sky ahead. I've let you sleep as long as I could.' Her voice sounded quite proud.

John looked to the south-east. He had been asleep for a long time. Across the dark sky a bright light shone from one side to the other, and then disappeared. After a few seconds the light went round again.

'That must be on land,' John said. 'It must be a lighthouse.'

'That must be on land. It must be a lighthouse.'

As they sailed on, the light seemed to be not so bright as before. At first John couldn't understand. Could the light go away from them? And then he understood. It wasn't as dark as before. Over in the east the morning light was coming. And when it came, they might be able to see land. But where? France . . . Belgium . . . Holland? Certainly somewhere they had never seen before.

Susan was busy making coffee and Roger and Titty were awake.

'Can't we get up now?' came Roger's voice.

'Breakfast first,' said Susan.

Ten minutes later they were all in the cockpit again.

'Where's the land?' asked Susan.

'Straight ahead,' said John.

'Shouldn't we turn back now?' said Susan. 'It's nearly daylight, and the wind isn't so strong. I'm sure I won't be seasick this time. And we've absolutely got to get back.'

John looked at her. 'I've been thinking,' he said. 'I don't think we should turn back at all, Susan. The wind's still behind us. We've been sailing all night and we've come a long way. It's going to take a long time to go back; longer against the wind. The most important thing is to tell Mother where we are. Today's the day we promised to be back. We can't do that. We must tell Mother and Jim where we are.'

'But how?' asked Susan.

'We'll go on and get into a harbour and send a telegram to Mother.'

'And perhaps Jim Brading could come to take us home,' said Susan, her voice full of hope. 'Yes. We'd better go on.'

The thing had been decided. From that moment not one of them looked back, not even Susan. They hadn't meant to go to sea, but here they were, and there was an unknown land ahead. Slowly the orange light in the east grew brighter and brighter, like a golden fire, and then the sun rose, round and bright. The sea was no longer grey; it was blue and green. But there was no land in sight. The new day had started and the *Goblin* was still alone in the middle of an empty sea.

'I think we can put more sail on,' said John. 'Then the *Goblin* will sail faster to the land.'

'What's that in the water?' said Roger suddenly.

'It's a big piece of wood,' said John. 'It probably fell from a ship in the storm. There's another. We've got to be careful. We don't want to hit anything.'

There was a lot of wood around them now, and then Roger shouted, 'That's like a box. And there's something on it. Oh, oh, it's a little cat. It's dead.'

'Oh . . . Poor thing!' said Titty sadly.

They could just see it, a small wet brown body on top of the box. 'How terrible,' said Susan. 'It was probably asleep on the box when it fell into the water.'

'It's alive,' shouted Roger. 'I saw its mouth open.'

And as they passed the wooden box and the wet brown body of the cat, they saw a pink mouth open again, just a little. The baby cat was whispering a cry for help, but they could not hear it.

'We must save it,' cried Titty.

John was already pulling in the mainsail. 'Susan, take the tiller. Roger, don't lose sight of the box. Don't take your eyes off it!'

The mainsail swung across, and the *Goblin* turned and came closer to the box in the water.

'Hold on to my feet,' said John. In another second it would be too late. John bent down from the side of the

In another second it would be too late.

cockpit with both hands held out, while Titty and Susan held on to his legs. Just as the wooden box passed on the waves, John caught the cold, wet body of the little cat. Titty and Susan pulled, and slowly John's body came back into the cockpit. The little cat was in his hands. John gave it to Susan, took the tiller again, and turned the *Goblin* back on her course. He had his captain's job to do. The little cat lay still in Susan's hands, too exhausted and too cold to move.

'We'll take it down into the cabin and get it warm and dry. We've got a bottle of milk, too,' said Susan.

Roger put some milk onto a saucer and Titty held the cat's head close to the milk. It opened its mouth and a thin pink tongue came out, and went in again. The cat couldn't move its head enough. Susan put a drop of milk on her finger and held it to the cat's mouth. Again the little tongue came out and this time the cat took the milk, and opened its mouth for more. After a few minutes, with more milk from Susan's finger, the little cat opened its eyes and closed them again. Then it opened its mouth and made a small noise . . . miaow.

'It's going to be all right,' said Roger.

'Let's call it Sinbad,' said Titty. 'Like Sinbad the Sailor in the story.'

She and Roger went on giving Sinbad milk while Susan went up on deck to help John put on more sail. Overhead there was a lot of banging and shouting for a while, and then suddenly the *Goblin* was moving faster through the water. Sinbad, now warm and dry and full of milk, took a few careful steps along the floor.

Just then John's face appeared at the cabin door.

'Come and look,' he called. 'We've got fishing boats ahead.' Roger and Titty, carrying their new passenger with

Sinbad took a few careful steps along the floor.

48

them, came up into the cockpit. The *Goblin*, with all her sails up, was hurrying along over a blue sea in bright sunshine.

A long way away they could see a lot of fishing boats – but they weren't like any fishing boats they had ever seen before.

'They aren't English, are they?' said Roger.

'No, the sails aren't like English sails at all,' said John. 'I think they're Dutch. Land can't be far away. I'm going to climb the mast to see.'

'No . . . No,' said Susan, but already John was at the bottom of the mast and climbing, holding on to the ropes. The three children held their breath as they watched.

'Land! Land ahead!' came the happy shout when John reached the top of the mast. 'Land straight ahead!'

Soon even from the cockpit they could see the lighthouse ahead. John came down from the top of the mast and told them there was also a ship ahead, but it wasn't moving. It seemed to be anchored.

'We've got to find out where we are,' he said, 'and I'm going to ask, but first I've got to make everything tidy on deck.' He put all the ropes and sails in good order and came back to the cockpit. Ahead of them the ship grew larger and larger, but didn't move. Suddenly John shouted.

'It's a pilot ship! It's all right. We can ask for a pilot to show us the way into the nearest harbour. Quick, let's get the flag up.'

Hurriedly, they found the right flag – a blue and white

square one, which was the sign asking for a pilot to come on board. John pulled it up on a rope to the top of the mast.

'But what land do you think it'll be?' asked Roger. 'And what language will the pilot speak?'

'I know a little French,' said John, 'but not much.'

'John,' said Susan suddenly, 'do you remember what Jim said about people having to pay a lot of money if they need help at sea? What will happen if the pilot realizes that we're only children and that we don't know where we are? Perhaps he'll take the *Goblin* away and Jim will have to pay a lot of money to get her back.'

'But Jim hasn't got a lot of money,' said Titty. 'He told us. Perhaps we'd better not have a pilot after all.'

'We *must* have one,' said Susan, 'because we have to get into a harbour safely and send a telegram to Mother.'

They were now quite near the pilot ship and a small rowing boat was coming from it towards the *Goblin*.

'Look,' said John. 'There's only one thing to do. We mustn't let the pilot think there are only children aboard. We've got to pretend that everything is perfectly normal. I'll stay up here and steer, and you all go down into the cabin and shut the door.'

'Do we pretend not to be there?' asked Titty.

'No. No,' said John. 'Make a noise – a lot of adult kind of noise, so that the pilot thinks there's a captain and a crew in the cabin.'

'Shall I play my whistle?' asked Roger hopefully. Usually the others told him to be quiet when he played his whistle.

'Shall I play my whistle?' asked Roger.

'Good idea,' said John. 'You can't tell how old a person is by listening to a penny whistle. And make a noise with your feet, and bang plates and things together. Try and sound like an adult party.'

The others hurried down into the cabin.

A few minutes later, with John alone at the tiller, the pilot, a big, red-faced man, arrived on board.

'Good day, mynheer,' said the pilot, reaching for the tiller. 'You want me to take you into Flushing?'

'Yes, please,' said John, very happy that the pilot spoke English.

'Where are you from?' asked the pilot.

'Harwich,' replied John, wondering why the others in the cabin were so silent.

'Your captain chose bad weather to come across from Harwich in this little boat.'

John said nothing. He didn't know what to say to this strange, friendly man.

'Little boat,' said the pilot, 'but very good.'

And then John heard, at last, the sound of Roger's whistle, and singing and other loud noises from the cabin.

'Your captain has a party,' said the pilot, smiling. 'He is happy, after his stormy crossing.'

John watched, trying to think of something to say, as the *Goblin* sailed past a number of big buoys in the water. They were coming closer and closer to the land.

'Where do you want to go, mynheer?' said the pilot. 'Now, go and call your captain.'

John shook his head. He did not know what to do. They would have to pay the pilot. They would need money to send a telegram to Mother. They had only about two English pounds with them, and there were too many questions to answer at once.

Down in the cabin Roger was playing 'Swanee River' on his whistle, very badly.

The pilot laughed. 'Your captain gave orders not to annoy him? A very hard man! I had a captain like that when I was very young. So, we go on without him.'

The *Goblin* went on through the mouth of the harbour and suddenly they were sailing past a big black ship that was getting ready to leave.

'That boat's going to Harwich,' said the pilot. 'The ferry from Flushing to Harwich. It's leaving now.'

John looked up at the high black side of the Dutch ferry. There were several passengers looking over the side, and suddenly John saw a face he knew – a face filled with surprise, looking down at him.

'AHOY THERE! JOHN! The shout rang over the water.

'It's Daddy,' whispered John, then he shouted, 'Ahoy!

Suddenly John saw a face he knew.

Ahoy!' But the passenger on the ferry had disappeared.

'Fine voice,' said the pilot. 'A sailor's voice. You know him?'

'Yes,' said John sadly. Why hadn't the *Goblin* arrived ten minutes earlier?

'Very fast ship,' said the pilot. 'They will be in England

very soon. But now we make a surprise for your captain. There is our buoy. We stop there.'

And John ran forward, put the rope through the ring on the buoy, and the *Goblin* came safely to a stop.

'Good,' said the pilot. 'Now we call your captain,' and he banged his hand hard on the roof of the cabin, shouting, 'Now CAPTAIN!' at the top of his voice.

The seventeenth repeat of 'Swanee River' came to a sudden stop.

6
Arriving in Holland

S usan pushed the cabin door open. They saw the Dutch pilot looking at them.

'How do you do?' said Susan.

'Can we come out now?' came Roger's voice.

'Susan,' said John, 'Daddy's on that ferry going out of the harbour. He saw us, and shouted, but it was too late.'

'Daddy! Oh no! It can't be.'

They crowded up into the cockpit and watched miserably as the big black ferry left the harbour to go across the sea to Harwich. The pilot was looking past them down into the cabin.

'So many children,' he said. 'But where is the captain?'

John looked at Susan, but said nothing. He could not

think of anything to say. It was Susan who spoke.

'We'd better tell you everything,' she said. 'There isn't a captain. At least John is, really. You see, we didn't really mean to come to sea. We didn't mean to come all the way across the North Sea. And now we have to send a telegram and ask Mother to send us some money, so that we can pay you.'

'No captain?' said the pilot. 'No captain! Four children . . . and a small cat!'

'We saved Sinbad on the way,' said Titty.

'Four children alone . . . and you crossed the North Sea, in last night's storm. Not even I would cross the North Sea in so small a boat.'

And the pilot took John's arm. 'You, all alone, you brought this little boat all that way, in that bad weather? There is not one boy in Holland who can do that!'

As the pilot was speaking, the children heard the noise of a motorboat coming across the harbour towards the *Goblin*.

'AHOY!' came an English voice. The little motorboat was very close to the *Goblin* now, and sitting in it was . . .

'DADDY!' shouted all four children together.

In another moment he was aboard.

'Hello!' said Daddy. 'Whose boat is this? I never thought that someone might bring you across to meet me.'

'We didn't mean to go to sea,' said Susan.

'It was in the fog,' said John.

'We couldn't help it, really,' said Susan, and looking at Daddy she knew that everything was all right now. It was too much for her. Tears started to run down her face, and she ran into the cabin.

'Across the North Sea!' said the pilot. 'Alone! Alone across the North Sea! I do not believe it, but it is true – four children came across the North Sea alone in last night's storm!'

'Daddy, have you got plenty of money?' said Roger. 'Susan wants to send a telegram to Mother, and we haven't paid the pilot.'

'Of course,' said Daddy as he turned to the pilot. 'What is the cost of your work to bring this big boat into Flushing?'

The pilot banged his hand down hard on to his knee.

'Nothing! Nothing at all! You have very fine children, Sir, and I will take nothing from you. But I will take you into the inner harbour. Then you can send your telegram.'

'I can't believe it's Daddy really,' said Titty, as the *Goblin* moved into the inner harbour at Flushing.

'Of course it is,' said Roger.

'I know,' said Titty, 'but I still can't believe it.'

It had been a long time since they had last seen him, but Daddy had not changed a bit. He was always calm, and didn't seem at all surprised to find his four children on a little yacht in a Dutch harbour. And while the pilot was with them, Daddy would ask them no questions. Susan wanted very much to explain everything to him, but first they had to send that telegram to Mother.

In the inner harbour there were lots of small boats, all

clean and tidy, and the pilot took them over to an empty place beside another pilot ship, just like the one they had seen outside Flushing harbour.

The pilot shook hands with all of them, but twice with John. 'I will bring you charts,' he said, 'for the North Sea, for your journey home. I have plenty. I will see you later, captain,' he said to John, and then he was gone.

'Daddy, what about that telegram?' said Susan.

'We've got to think about what we're going to say. But first, you'd better tell me all about it,' said Daddy. 'Come on,' and he opened the door to the cabin. 'Let's go down below.'

'Jim Brading? Never heard of him,' said Daddy.

The children were finding it difficult to tell Daddy that Mother knew nothing about what had happened. They didn't know what had happened to the owner of the *Goblin*. It was even more difficult to explain how they had sailed into Flushing just as he was leaving on the ferry to Harwich.

'Mother will be terribly worried,' said Susan.

'Jim, too,' said John.

'He will, poor man,' said Daddy. 'We've got to hope that he's been too worried to tell her. Perhaps something happened to keep him ashore.'

Daddy thought for a few minutes.

'I know what we'll do. We've got to let your Mother

know you're all right. But we don't want her to worry, so we shan't say anything about the North Sea. So the telegram mustn't come from Holland.'

'But we must send one,' said Susan.

'We will,' said Daddy, 'but I'll send it first to a friend of mine at Shotley, and ask him to send it to your Mother at Pin Mill. She'll think it's come from Shotley and that you're there. She won't be very pleased with you, but I can't do anything about that. And now, we'd better go and find the Post Office to send the telegram.'

The children had been on the moving deck of a yacht for so long that at first they found it difficult to walk straight on dry land. They walked slowly through streets with tables outside the cafés and people wearing strange clothes. They reached the Post Office at last and Daddy sent the telegram.

'Nothing more we can do now,' he said, as they came out again into the fresh air, 'and we've got two hours before the tide turns and we can sail back. What about something to eat?'

'A good idea, Daddy,' said Roger happily.

'Thought you might like it,' said Daddy. 'Come on.'

They found a café with tables outside, and sat down. Suddenly all the children realized that it was a long, long time since they had eaten. They were very hungry and they ate very well. Then John found that his eyes were closing, but he woke up again to help tell Daddy how they had saved Sinbad, the baby cat, from the sea.

They bought some bread and milk for the voyage back to

Harwich, and also five pairs of Dutch wooden shoes – a pair for each of the children and a fifth pair as a present for Bridget back at home. Then they found their way back to the *Goblin*. The Dutch pilot was there, with a crowd of Dutch children.

'I have told these boys and girls,' the pilot said, 'that you sailed in this little boat all the way across the North Sea in last night's storm. They didn't believe me. But now they can see you, and they must believe me.'

With the pilot's help, Daddy bought fresh water, petrol for the engine, and oil for the ship's lights, and soon they were ready to go.

The Dutch pilot was there, with a crowd of Dutch children.

59

As the *Goblin* sailed out of the harbour there was a loud shout of 'Goodbye . . . Goodbye, English,' from the Dutch children, and the pilot waved goodbye, too.

The *Goblin* was a happier ship now that she was on her way home. She was not going on and on into unknown seas, and everybody on board wanted her to go home just as fast as she could. Although they had sent a telegram to Mother, they still felt badly when they thought of her waiting for them at Pin Mill. They left the land of Holland behind them and sailed on, as it slowly became dark again.

They had bought petrol but after a while Daddy said, 'Roger. Go and turn off the engine. We can sail just as fast without it. And now, it's time for bed, all of you. Roger and Titty first.'

'I'm not a bit sleepy,' said Roger, but orders were orders, and two minutes after he went to bed, he was fast asleep. Titty had Sinbad to take care of, but both of them went to sleep very quickly, too. Susan had prepared a good, hot dinner for everybody, and had even been able to eat her part of it without feeling seasick. She was tired, but so happy that Daddy was with them now. With Daddy everything would be all right. Susan, too, fell asleep very quickly.

John, the captain, sat in the cockpit, holding the tiller, while Daddy studied the charts and planned the way back to Harwich. How much easier it was, John thought, when you had someone else to tell you where to go. When his father came up on deck again, John said,

'I could go on all night.'

'I expect you could,' said Commander Walker, 'but I think you need some sleep. You've done your bit. And I've been sitting in a train doing nothing for days and days. It's time to go to bed. Now, good night, John.'

John was quickly in bed, but he lay awake for a few minutes, thinking about how lucky they had been. And Daddy seemed almost pleased with them. Daddy seemed to think they had done rather well. And then, John, too, fell asleep as the *Goblin* sailed back across the North Sea towards England.

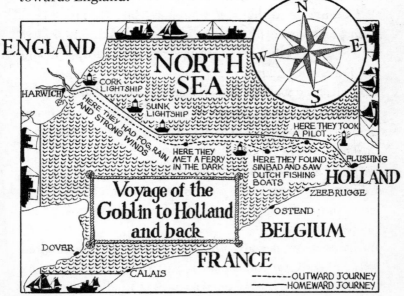

7
Coming home

There was bright sunlight in the cabin when the children heard Daddy shout, 'Time to get up now!'

Daylight already . . .

They all climbed quickly out of bed, trying to wake up and get into their clothes at the same time. When they came up on deck, the sun was shining, and ahead of them they could see a lightship.

'Where are we?' asked John.

'Coming up to the *Sunk* lightship,' said Daddy. 'Here, John, you take the tiller. Susan, what about some breakfast? And Roger, get the engine ready. The wind's dropping and we'll need the engine.'

By the time they had finished breakfast, the *Sunk* was far behind them, and the engine was pushing the *Goblin* faster towards Harwich. Soon they saw land and then . . .

'That's the Beach End buoy.'

'We saw that . . . in the fog,' said Roger.

'That's how we knew we were at sea,' said John.

Jim Brading woke up. Where was he? He remembered some things – someone putting him to bed, someone giving him food to eat, but where was he? He tried to sit up, and found that he had the most terrible headache.

The door opened and a nurse came in.

'Ah, you're awake. That's better,' she said. 'Now, just lie there until the doctor comes.'

Jim looked at her. 'Doctor? What doctor? Where am I?'

'In hospital,' said the nurse. 'And you've been very lucky. The doctor says you've got a good hard head.'

And she went out of the room.

Jim put his hands up to feel his head, which was covered in thick bandages. What had happened to him? He remembered that he had come to get petrol for the *Goblin*. But he couldn't buy any around the harbour, and he had to catch the bus to go to the nearest petrol station. He remembered an old lady in front of him, and then . . . nothing else.

And then he remembered the four Walker children, aboard his *Goblin*, by themselves. And he had promised Mrs Walker that he would take care of them. He got up. He had to go, at once. But something was still banging in his head and the room wouldn't keep still. It was like a boat in a storm. And where were his clothes?

In a small cupboard in that white hospital room Jim found his clothes and put them on. Slowly and carefully he walked out of the room and towards the outside door. Nobody stopped him and in a few minutes he was outside the hospital, standing in the street.

A bus came along, stopped, and Jim climbed in.

'I'm glad to see you're all right,' said the driver. 'And

Bill will be glad, too. He thought he'd killed you when you ran right in front of his bus.'

And Jim began to understand why he had woken up in hospital. But how long had he been there?

The bus arrived at the harbour. Jim got out and looked across the water for the *Goblin*. He looked again, and again. She had gone.

He looked up and down the harbour. The *Goblin* wasn't there. Jim half-walked, half-ran along to where he had moored his dinghy when he left the *Goblin* to get petrol. What should he do? Should he telephone Mrs Walker at Pin Mill? That was no good if the *Goblin* was already at Pin Mill, and much worse if she wasn't there. What could he do?

For an hour or more he hurried around the harbour, desperately asking everyone he knew, 'Where's the *Goblin*? Have you seen the *Goblin*?' He heard about the fog and the storm, and realized that he had been in hospital for two days and two nights. But no one had any news of the *Goblin*.

He went back to his little dinghy, his head aching, and knew he would have to go and tell Mrs Walker.

'Ahoy there!' Jim looked around. A motorboat was coming along quite fast, and someone shouted, 'We heard you were looking for your yacht. She's just coming in now from the *Cork* lightship,' and the man pointed out to sea.

Jim looked, and saw a white boat, red sails . . . the *Goblin*, coming in from the open sea. But how could that

Jim looked, and saw a white boat, red sails . . .

be? His head hurt, and he could not think clearly. But there was the *Goblin* coming in to harbour, and her desperate owner rowed to meet her.

'BEACH END!'

The children read the name on the buoy as they sailed past it. The last time it had meant that everything was wrong. Now it meant that everything was going to be all right. Nothing could be wrong with Daddy sitting there holding the tiller.

A motorboat came towards them. 'Where are you from?' shouted a voice.

Daddy whispered to John, 'You're the captain. Tell them you've come from Flushing, in Holland.'

'Flushing,' shouted John. 'In Holland.'

'We'll need to come aboard,' shouted the man in the Customs boat.

'We'll stop inside Shotley Spit,' shouted John.

'All right. We'll see you there.'

'There's another boat ahead,' called Roger. 'It's got a man in it with a strange white thing round his head.'

All the children looked and John cried, 'It's Jim Brading!'

'Is that the young man who lost you?' asked Daddy. 'By the look of him, he's been in trouble. Someone or something's hit him on the head. We'll stop and bring him on board.'

As the little dinghy arrived, with Jim Brading looking quite ill, but at the same time very pleased, the children all started talking at once.

'We didn't mean to go to sea . . . This is Daddy . . . I've lost your anchor and chain . . . We drifted away in the fog . . . We couldn't get back . . . What's the matter with your head? . . . Quick, Daddy, he's ill . . .'

Commander Walker was just in time to catch Jim as he tried to climb into the *Goblin*.

'He's had a bit of a shock,' said Daddy. 'Leave him alone. Don't ask questions.' And then Daddy himself asked Jim the most important question of all.

'Does my wife know?'

Jim looked at them all. At first it seemed that he hadn't understood the question. But then his lips moved . . . 'I couldn't tell her,' he said slowly. 'They put me in hospital. I only got away this morning.'

Immediately, John and Susan and the younger children felt better. They knew that Mother would be worried about them, but at least she didn't know what had really happened.

By now they were in the middle of Harwich harbour. The Customs man came and talked to them, and checked the ship's papers, and then it was time to go to Pin Mill and meet Mother.

'Look here,' said Daddy. 'The tide's turning. We can't sail up the river against the tide. Let's get everything really tidy, and then we'll use the engine to take us up river. We want everything to look good when we meet your mother.'

Everyone, except Jim, got to work and soon they were ready to go.

'Susan,' said Daddy, 'what about inviting Mother and Bridget to eat aboard the *Goblin*? Can you get us a meal ready?'

'I got a meal ready for you all last night,' said Susan

proudly, 'out in the middle of the North Sea. I think I can manage to get one ready on the river.'

'Of course you can,' replied Daddy.

As they sailed up the river to Pin Mill, Susan got the meal ready while Daddy spoke to Jim Brading in the cabin and

They sailed up the river to Pin Mill.

68

John was again the captain of the *Goblin*. But when they got near Pin Mill, Jim came up out of the cabin.

'I'm going to take her in,' he said.

'There's Mother and Bridget,' shouted Roger.

Suddenly Daddy hid below the cabin top. 'Look,' he said, 'I don't want to give her too many surprises at once. Can you manage without me?'

'I'll take her in,' said Jim Brading, 'and John can catch the buoy – he knows what to do. But I don't know what I'm going to say to Mrs Walker.'

The *Goblin* came quietly and slowly up to her buoy. John reached down, caught the buoy and tied the rope to fix the *Goblin* safely to her mooring. Jim disappeared back down into the cabin.

'Mother's got a dinghy,' cried Titty. 'She's coming to meet us.'

'Don't try to tell her everything at once,' said Daddy from his hiding-place in the cabin.

As Mother came nearer, the four children were thinking of everything they had to tell her. It was a good thing she hadn't known that they had been to sea alone, and that Jim had been in hospital. But she would have to know now. How could they tell her? They had all promised not to go to sea. And they had all promised to be back in time for tea yesterday.

Mrs Walker stopped her dinghy before she reached the *Goblin*. She spoke very quietly, but they all knew at once that she was very angry.

'John, Susan, didn't you promise that you would be back yesterday? I wish now I hadn't let you go. I know it was a stormy night, but why didn't you come back yesterday by bus from Shotley?'

'But we couldn't,' said John.

'We weren't at Shotley at all,' said Roger.

'I had a telegram from Daddy yesterday,' Mummy went on. 'One from Berlin. And another one from Flushing. He must be on his way now. And nobody to meet him!'

Jim's head in its white bandages came up from the cabin. 'It wasn't their fault, Mrs Walker,' he said. 'It was all mine.'

'What are all those wooden shoes?' said Bridget.

'What have you done to your head, Jim?' said Mrs Walker. 'Have you had an accident? You were quite right not to sail if you were ill. But why didn't the children come home from Shotley by bus? And why didn't you telephone? A telegram didn't explain anything. And Daddy is probably waiting, wondering why there's nobody to meet him.'

'He knows all about it,' cried Titty. 'And he thinks you'll like Sinbad . . . Oh, where *is* Sinbad?'

The little cat had climbed out of the cabin and was walking across the cabin roof.

'Oh, look, Mummy!' cried Bridget. 'They've got a cat.'

Mother looked away from her naughty children. She had been so worried, first in the fog and then in the storm. And after that, they hadn't come home. They sent her a telegram, and they had broken all their promises. It was too much. She watched the little cat walk along by the side of the cabin, and then she saw something else. A hand, a thin brown hand, came out of the cabin window and caught Sinbad.

'Ted!' she cried.

Daddy's head appeared out of the cabin.

'Hello, Mary,' said Daddy. 'Don't be too hard on them. They didn't mean to go to sea.'

'I'm coming aboard,' said Mother. 'You naughty children. Why did you go to meet Daddy in Harwich? That wasn't very nice for Bridget and me.'

'No,' said Roger, unable to miss his chance. 'No . . . We met him in Holland.'

'Don't be silly,' said Mother as she climbed aboard. 'You've been very naughty, and I don't think I should kiss any of you.'

'You should kiss them all,' said Daddy. 'Believe me, they've earned it.'

'Oh well,' said Mother. 'If Jim had an accident, I suppose it wasn't completely their fault. But we were *all* going to meet you, not just these four naughty children on their own.'

'But Mother, didn't you hear?' said Roger. 'We didn't meet him in Harwich – we met him in Holland.'

'Oh yes,' said Mother, who clearly thought that this was one of Roger's jokes.

'Now Mary,' said Daddy. 'We've got a meal nearly ready for you in the cabin, and everybody wants you and Bridget to have lunch on the *Goblin*.'

'We'd love to do that,' said Mother. 'But we've got to tell Miss Powell first, so that she knows we won't be in for lunch.'

Roger wasn't going to forget about Holland.

'Don't you understand, Mother? We really did meet him in Holland.'

'Don't you understand, Mother?
We really did meet him in Holland.'

'Oh yes,' laughed Mother. 'And I suppose you bought those wooden shoes yourselves in a Dutch shop.'

'Yes, they did,' said Daddy, and Mother, looking at his face, saw that he meant it.

'Jim!' said Mother. 'You promised me that you wouldn't take my children out of the harbour. How could you take them right across the North Sea, in that terrible weather?'

'I . . . I . . .' said Jim, and put a hand to his head. This was all too much for him.

'Jim wasn't there,' said Daddy. 'And I've got to telephone the hospital about him. And you've got to tell Miss Powell about lunch. Come with me, Mary, and I'll tell you all about it. Lunch'll be ready when we get back.'

A moment later he and Mother were gone, and the four children watched as Daddy rowed their mother ashore and told her all about it.

'It's going to be all right,' said Titty.

'Yes,' said Susan. 'Daddy'll tell her that we didn't mean to go to sea.'

73

Exercises

A Checking your understanding

Chapters 1 and 2 *Who in these chapters . . .*
1 . . . tied the *Goblin*'s rope to the buoy?
2 . . . was on his way home from China?
3 . . . went with Mrs Walker to get food in Ipswich?
4 . . . was steering when Roger saw the porpoise?
5 . . . started the *Goblin*'s engine?
6 . . . didn't come back for his breakfast?

Chapters 3 and 4 *Write answers to these questions.*
1 What had changed in the six hours since Jim had left?
2 Why didn't the kedge anchor hold on the bottom of the sea?
3 Why did John decide to put up the sails?
4 Why did they have to turn the *Goblin* round again and go on?
5 Why did John go along the roof of the cabin to the mast?
6 Why did Susan scream?

Chapters 5 and 6 *Are these sentences true (T) or false (F)?*
1 John fell asleep while he was steering.
2 Roger steered the *Goblin* while John slept.
3 The pilot thought that John was the captain of the *Goblin*.
4 The pilot wouldn't take any money for his work.
5 Daddy sent the telegram to a friend at Shotley.
6 John sailed the *Goblin* back across the North Sea.

Chapter 7 *Find answers to these questions in the text.*
1 Why was Jim Brading in hospital?
2 Why did Daddy hide when the *Goblin* arrived at Pin Mill?
3 Why was Mrs Walker so angry?
4 How did Mrs Walker learn that her husband was on the *Goblin*?
5 What did Mother think was one of Roger's jokes?

B Working with language

1 *Complete these sentences with information from the story.*
1 Jim Brading fell asleep on the dinner table because . . .
2 The first morning Jim was in a hurry to set sail so . . .
3 The children knew they were out at sea when . . .
4 Although Susan and Titty were seasick, . . .
5 The children decided to sail on into a harbour so that . . .

2 *Put Sinbad's story into the right order and make five sentences.*
1 John at once began to turn the *Goblin* around.
2 Titty and Susan held on to John's legs
3 and soon it opened its eyes and made a small noise.
4 The *Goblin* was sailing along happily
5 but then he saw its pink mouth open.
6 as he bent down and caught the cold, wet body of the little cat.
7 when Roger saw a little cat on a box in the sea.
8 Susan gave the cat some milk on her finger
9 Although they could not hear the cat crying for help,
10 At first he thought the little cat on the box was dead,

C Activities

1 Imagine that you are one of the children. Write a letter to a
school friend, describing your adventure at sea.
2 What do you think Commander Walker said to his wife after
they left the *Goblin* together at Pin Mill? Write down their
conversation.
3 Which do *you* think is the most exciting or interesting way to
travel? By car or bus, by plane (large or small), small sailing boat
or a large ship, on foot, on horseback, by bicycle? Write a few
lines saying which way you would choose and why.

Glossary

Ahoy   a word used by seamen to call attention

Aye, aye, sir   'yes, sir', said by sailors to an order on a ship

course   the way (north, west, etc.) a ship is going

crew   the group of people who work together on a ship

drift   to move slowly and without a plan

ferry   a boat that takes people across a river or sea

harbour   a place where ships can stop safely next to land

joke   a funny story that makes you laugh

moor   to tie a ship to something to keep it in one place

naughty   behaving badly, making trouble

navy   all the warships of a country

pier   a wall from the land into the sea, where people can get on and off boats

pilot   someone who guides a ship the safe way into a harbour

point   to show with your arm or finger where something is

pump   a machine that moves water into or out of something

shoal   a shallow place in the sea

shock   a very big, sudden surprise (often not a nice one)

sink   to go down under water

starboard   the side of a ship which is on the right when you are looking forward

steer   to move something (a tiller, a wheel) which guides a boat, car, etc.

swing (past tense **swung**)   to move from side to side, or backwards and forwards

telegram   a message sent quickly by electricity or radio

tide   the rise and fall of the sea that happens twice a day